Smiley's DreamBook

a BONE tale by Jeff Smith

COLOR BY TOM GAADT

SCHOLASTIC INC.

ISBN 978-1-338-31955-2

12 11 10 9 8 7 6 5 4 3 2 1   19 20 21 22 23 24

Printed in the U.S.A.   169

This edition first printing, January 2019

Book design by Jeff Smith and Steve Ponzo

Jeff Smith is the award-winning creator of the *New York Times* bestselling BONE series. This epic story about three Bone cousins lost in a valley filled with wonderful and terrifying creatures is loved by readers young and old, and was named by *Time* as one of the top ten graphic novels of all time. Today, there are millions of BONE books in print in the United States, and they have been translated into thirty languages worldwide.

Smith started drawing stories about the BONE characters before the age of ten. In 1991, he launched the comic book BONE and began to create the serialized epic fantasy story that was eventually published in nine volumes. Jeff was the subject of a documentary called *The Cartoonist: Jeff Smith, BONE, and the Changing Face of Comics.*

Jeff lives (and dreams) in Columbus, Ohio, with his wife, Vijaya Iyer. Visit him online at boneville.com.